The Wondrous Works of God

ILLUSTRATED BY SYMEON SHIMIN

Materials for Christian Education
Prepared at the Direction of General Convention

The Seabury Press • Greenwich, Connecticut

THE SEABURY SERIES is prepared for Christian education in parishes and missions by the National Council
of the Protestant Episcopal Church in the United States
of America at the direction of the General Convention.

THE REV. DAVID R. HUNTER, ED.D.
    Director
    Department of Christian Education

THE REV. WILLIAM SYDNOR, M.A.
    Executive Secretary
    Division of Curriculum Development

LIBRARY OF CONGRESS CATALOGUE CARD NUMBER: 56-7849

PRINTED IN THE UNITED STATES OF AMERICA AT THE LAKESIDE PRESS
R. R. DONNELLEY & SONS COMPANY, CHICAGO, AND CRAWFORDSVILLE, INDIANA

The
Wondrous Works
of God

Jock Kent Has a Fall

O all ye Powers of the Lord, bless ye the Lord:
praise him, and magnify him for ever.

It was a sunny-muddy afternoon in March. Jock Kent ran up the path toward home. Jock was seven years old. He had a mother and father, three big brothers, Tom, Seth, and Oliver, and a dog with flappy ears named Scoop.

Jock couldn't decide whether to play outside or inside.

Just as he was opening the front door he remembered his cousin Sylvia! Mum was bringing her from town for a long visit. They might come driving up any minute, and he hadn't even started a WELCOME sign.

Jock pulled off his jacket, found paper and crayons, and set to work. Cars whizzed by and any one of them might stop and there would be Mum and Sylvia.

It would be much better to wait for them outside. He zipped up his jacket and hurried out to look down the road. Jock climbed up on Scoop's kennel for a better view. Seth, his sixteen-year-old brother, came along.

"I wish they'd hurry up and come," Jock said.

"Sylvia may not get here for a long time," Seth said. "Why don't you go and play next door?"

Jock shook his head and jumped down from the kennel. "Nope. If I stay here I'll see them sooner."

"O.K. You're the chief welcomer," Seth said as he went toward the house.

Jock began to draw a star in the driveway mud with his toe. Sure he was chief welcomer. Sylvia was almost his age. He'd be eight in June and she would be eight in August. Jock loved stars, especially the Big Dipper. Maybe Sylvia would like stars, too. His big brothers knew a lot about the sky and everything. He would, too, when he was as old as they were.

Jock grinned as he pulled his toe through the soft, squishy mud. If the star looked like

a star he would print WELCOME in the mud below it. That would be better than any old indoor WELCOME sign.

Jock could hardly wait for his cousin to arrive. He was almost glad that Sylvia's mother and father had moved to Australia. It meant that his favorite cousin would live with them for a long, long time—until her mother and father found a house to live in. Mum had shown him on the globe just where Australia was. It was all the way around on the other side of the world.

Jock's star turned out lop-sided. Maybe Sylvia wouldn't like stars, anyway. He'd make a circle for the earth. On top he'd put a mark for the United States, and on the bottom he'd put a mark for Australia. He found if he stood on one foot and pulled his other foot around himself in a circle he could make a fine earth.

He knew Sylvia would like his sign. She'd like his school, too, and his church. She was going to the second grade with him on weekdays. She was going to St. Paul's Church on Sundays. She was going to do all the things you did when you lived in a place.

Jock grinned at the earth he had drawn in the mud. Now he'd better climb an apple tree and watch for the car. On the way up, a twig tickled his nose. Jock brushed it aside, sneezed, and fell right out of the tree!

He landed with a thump.

"Are you all right? Are you hurt?"

Jock looked up to see Dr. Gordon's familiar face. Dr. Gordon was rector of St. Paul's Church.

"I'm O.K.," Jock managed to say. He tried not to cry when Dr. Gordon helped him up.

Jock brushed some of the mud off his clothes.

"A scratchy old twig tickled me and made me sneeze. Then it pushed me right out of the tree."

"You weren't pushed," the rector said. "You were pulled. Right out of the tree onto the ground."

"Pulled?" Jock stared at him. "There wasn't anybody here."

"I didn't mean pulled by people. I meant pulled by the earth. This earth we live on. It pulled you right down to itself. We call that gravity. It's one of God's laws."

Jock forgot about being bumped and muddy. "Grav—ity? Gravity," he repeated. "What's that?"

"Are you too stiff to jump?" Dr. Gordon asked.

"Nope." Jock jumped good and high to show him.

"That's fine. Gravity is what pulled you back to the earth. If it hadn't, you would have gone spinning off into space."

"Hey, am I glad there's gravity!"

Dr. Gordon smiled. "So am I. God's law keeps things where they belong. Every single thing in God's whole wonderful universe obeys the law of gravity. Even people."

Jock looked over to the earth he had drawn in the mud. He'd tell Sylvia all about what he had just learned.

Jock heard the toot of a car horn. He saw Mum drive into the yard. "They've come! They've come!" he shouted and started to run.

A Lion in the Sky

O ye Winter and Summer, bless ye the Lord:
praise him, and magnify him for ever.

Sylvia was lonesome. It was nice of Aunt Matty
and Uncle John to invite her to stay with them,
but it would have been nicer if she were with
Mummy and Daddy in Australia. As she and
Jock's mother drove into the yard, Sylvia held
on tight to Rosie, her Teddy bear. It helped
to have something to hug.

14

Everything looked bare and empty. The country didn't look a bit like it had last summer when she and Mummy and Daddy stayed here for a week end.

Jock ran up to the car. "Hi, Sylvia," he shouted breathlessly. "Welcome! Wait till you see my sign. I made it all for you. It's the earth and . . ."

His mother opened the car door. "Jock, for goodness sake, calm down, and how did you get so dirty? Give your little cousin a chance to meet everyone again."

"She's not so little," Jock said quietly. "Hello, Sylvia."

"Hello, Jock." Sylvia tried to smile. She clung to her Teddy bear as she got out of the car.

Dr. Gordon came up the driveway.

"Hello, Dr. Gordon," Mrs. Kent said. "This is my niece, Sylvia Reed."

"Hello, Sylvia. I heard you were coming so I came to welcome you. I'm glad you are going to be here for a while."

Sylvia smiled but couldn't say a word.

"Well, I'll go along, Mrs. Kent," said Dr.

Gordon, "and come back when Sylvia is all settled."

"Please do," she answered.

Seth and Tom, Jock's big brothers, came running to say "hello." Scoop wagged his tail and waited for Sylvia to pet him.

Sylvia stared at the boys and Scoop. They

looked so different. Much bigger than they were last summer. Even Scoop seemed different.

"Seth and Tom, take Sylvia's suitcases to the house," their mother told them. "And you, Jock, go change your clothes—and scrub."

"When are we going to show Sylvia her room?" Jock asked.

"Right away. We want Sylvia to feel at home," his mother answered.

The big boys took their cousin's suitcases and Jock raced ahead to open the front door. "You'll like your room," he told Sylvia. "It's my biggest brother Oliver's room. He's in the Navy. I thought you'd like it because you can see the stars. You can see them better than from any room in the house."

Mrs. Kent put her arm around her niece as they entered Oliver's room. "We thought you'd like this room because it's close to all of us."

"It is nice," Sylvia said as she put Rosie down on the bed and walked to the window. It wasn't dark enough for stars. All she could see was leafless trees and tan fields. "If I look out there will I be looking toward Mummy and Daddy in Australia?" she asked.

"Well, sort of," Seth said. "Australia's right down under the other side of the world."

Jock interrupted excitedly. "I know that, too. Wait'll you see the WELCOME sign I made . . ."

"You can show it to Sylvia later, Jock," his mother said. "Tom, get the globe and show your cousin where Australia is."

"Seth and Tom are smart, but they're old," Jock told Sylvia. "Seth is sixteen and Tom is twelve."

Tom returned with the globe. "You're here," he said and put his finger on the United States. "And if you could look over and around the earth you'd be looking toward Australia. It's more than ten thousand miles away."

Sylvia felt farther away from Mummy and Daddy than ever.

"You can see the Big Dipper from here." Jock pointed to the window. "On every clear night. I wish I slept in this room."

"Can Mummy and Daddy see the Big Dipper in Australia?" Sylvia walked to the bed and picked up Rosie. "Can they?"

"No," Tom said. "They can't."

"Your mother and father can see the lion

in the sky, though, and so can you," Seth told her.

"Lion in the sky?" Sylvia looked puzzled.

"Yes," Seth smiled. "Leo-the-Lion. That's the name of a group of stars. After supper I'll show it to you."

Suddenly Sylvia knew she liked this big cousin very much.

Seth said, "Leo is part of our spring sky. Down under in Australia he's part of the fall sky because the seasons are just the opposite. It's fall there now."

Jock's mouth flew open. "You mean it's hot in winter and cold in summer?"

"Sure," Tom said.

"But how come?" Jock asked.

Seth started the globe spinning. As it spun he moved it slowly around the bulb of the desk lamp. "Pretend the light bulb is the sun," he said, "and this globe is the earth. The earth turns around once every twenty-four hours. When our part of the earth turns toward the sun we have daylight. When our part of the earth is turned away from the sun we have darkness."

"That's day and night. What makes summer and winter?" Jock asked.

Seth went on moving the globe around the light bulb. "Now watch this," he told them. "It takes the earth exactly a year to go around the sun." He put his finger on top of the globe. "When the North Pole tips toward the sun our part of the world has lots of sunlight, and that's our summer." He put his finger on the bottom of the globe. "When the South Pole tips toward the sun the North Pole tips away from

it. Then we have winter, and the people on the other half of the earth have summer."

"Gosh! Does God know about all this?"

"Why Jock, darling," Mrs. Kent's face was smiling. "God. . ."

She didn't get any further because Jock was jumping up and down saying, "God made it that way! Wow! God *made* it that way!"

"And another thing . . ." Seth started.

"That's enough for Sylvia and Jock to think about right now," Mrs. Kent told them. "I'll go downstairs and start supper."

They heard the front door open. "Where is everybody?" Mr. Kent called. "Where's my Sylvia?"

Jock rushed out, followed by Mrs. Kent and the older boys. Sylvia heard Jock shout: "Hi, Pop! Listen, I fell out of a tree and . . ."

Sylvia ran down the hall. Everybody seemed to have forgotten about her but she didn't mind. She was busy thinking.

Tonight she was going to see Leo-the-Lion. Mummy and Daddy, way down under in Australia, could too. Seth promised to show it to her. Sylvia didn't feel quite so lonesome any more. She was glad God had put a lion in the sky.

God's Great Compass

O ye Nights and Days, bless ye the Lord:
praise him, and magnify him for ever.

"Supper will be ready in ten minutes," Mum called out the kitchen window.

Jock ran to the house, followed by Sylvia. Jock was grinning happily because his cousin liked the WELCOME sign. She said she liked stars, too, just as much as he did.

"Is the table set?" Mum asked.

28

It was Jock's turn to set the table but he had forgotten. He started for the dining room. Seth caught him. "Scrub up first, you mud puppy," he said. "You'll get everything black."

"I'm scrubbed, and I used to set the table at home," Sylvia said. She showed Seth how clean her hands were. "And I'm taller than Jock so I can reach things better."

"Good girl!" Seth let go of his younger brother.

Jock pulled himself slowly up the stairs. He took three steps at a time. Maybe if he stretched enough he would grow quicker. His happiness was all gone and he felt cross because Sylvia was taller than he was. And cross because she liked setting tables. And especially cross because he knew he was being silly.

The cross feeling was all gone by the time

supper was over. They had had hamburgers and peas, which were Jock's favorites.

Mum said, "Let's all go out and see the stars. Then we'll come back and have hot chocolate and a surprise. We'll celebrate because Sylvia's here—and because Jock didn't get hurt when he fell out of the apple tree."

At eight o'clock they all put on coats and went out doors.

"There's the Big Dipper," Jock said and pointed. "It's got seven stars in it."

"A group of stars like that is called a constellation," Tom said. "Leo-the-Lion is a constellation too."

"A constellation is sort of a family of stars," Mum said. "Just like us. We are seven, now that Sylvia is here."

"That's right." Jock laughed. "We're just as many as the Big Dipper."

"But where is Leo-the-Lion?" Sylvia moved closer to Seth. "You promised to show me."

Seth laughed. "See the two stars at the front of the bowl of the Big Dipper?" Seth pointed them out as he spoke. "If you look *down* from those two front stars in the Dipper you'll come to Leo," he said. "In fact if the Dipper leaked it would drip right on him."

"I see a triangle and a question mark," Tom said. "They don't look much like a lion."

"Oh, I think I see it," said Sylvia jumping up and down in excitement. Turning to Mr. Kent, she asked, "Does anybody live on Leo? People like us?"

"Not on Leo or the moon," Mr. Kent said. "But there may be life somewhere else in the universe. Would you like to see the North star, Sylvia?"

"Oh, yes, show it to me," she said.

"Look again at the two stars at the front of the bowl of the Big Dipper. If you look *up* from those two stars you'll look right up to Polaris, the North Pole Star," Mr. Kent said.

"So you can find out where north is just by looking at those stars," Seth said.

"That's great! Then nobody can get lost, ever," Jock said.

Mr. Kent told them more about Polaris, the North Star. He explained how sailors steered their boats by it at night.

"That's because it shows them where north is," Jock said. "Just like a compass. Say, that's terrific! God's compass!"

"Yes, Jock," Dad told him. "God's great compass in the sky."

"Time for the hot chocolate and the surprise," Mum said and started for the house.

When the surprise was put on the table, Jock squealed with delight. Sylvia's eyes were as round as marbles. A whole box of little fancy cakes was before them.

When the last one was eaten it was time for Jock and Sylvia to go to bed.

After Jock had brushed his teeth and said his prayers, Mum tucked him in. Then she went across the hall and tucked in Sylvia.

When she left, Sylvia got up and knelt before the window. There was Leo. Maybe Mummy and Daddy were looking at it right now. And there was the North Star. Uncle John had called it God's great compass in the sky. Nobody could ever get lost. Mummy and Daddy wouldn't get lost. They'd be there in Australia waiting for her. Sylvia smiled when

she finished her prayers. Almost all the lone-
someness was gone now.

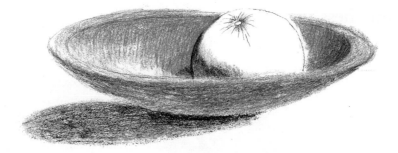

As Round as a Grapefruit!

O let the Earth bless the Lord: yea, let it praise him, and magnify him for ever.

The next morning when Sylvia went downstairs to breakfast, the sun was shining brightly. The red cherries in the dining-room wallpaper looked good enough to eat.

"Good morning," the Kents greeted her.

"Good morning," Sylvia answered as she sat down.

There was a bowl of fruit in the middle of the table. They all helped themselves. Mum went to the kitchen and came back with scrambled eggs and muffins. In a few minutes breakfast was all eaten up. Only a grapefruit was left.

"That grapefruit is as round as Tom's globe." Sylvia reached out and touched it. "Here's where we are. And here's Australia," she said as she touched the other side of the grapefruit.

"My, you've learned about the round world very quickly," Mrs. Kent said.

"I learned fast too," Jock said. "I knew all about it before Sylvia did."

Seth laughed and began to move the grape-

fruit around the light which hung down over the table. "Sylvia, pretend you're a little dot in Australia. Jock, you pretend you're a little dot in the United States," he told them. "Now pretend that bunch of cherries at the top of the wallpaper is Leo-the-Lion. Watch me as I turn the grapefruit."

Sylvia and Jock watched silently.

"Do you know why both of you dot people can see that bunch of cherries?" Seth answered his own question. "Because it's so high up and far away. That's the reason we can see Leo-the-Lion from here and so can people in Australia."

Tom held the stem from an apple close over the top of the grapefruit as Seth moved it. "Pretend the stem is the Big Dipper," he said. "And you can see why people on the other side of the grapefruit, that's Australia, couldn't see it. The grapefruit, which is the world, gets in the way."

"If you were really those little dots, you'd think the grapefruit was flat," Tom said.

"That's right," Seth said. "Just the way people thought our world was flat a long time ago."

A school bus tooted. Sylvia and the boys said good-by and hurried off.

Sylvia didn't think about being scared of her new school until she was walking through the playground past dozens of strange children.

"Hurry up!" Jock gave her arm a quick pull. "I want to tell our teacher about the grapefruit. Her name is Miss Marks."

"Why, hello, Sylvia." Miss Marks was waiting by the classroom door. "We're so glad to have you with us."

"Miss Marks, you know what?" Jock began. "Sylvia had the neatest idea about a grapefruit being the world. And Seth and Tom told us loads about the earth and the stars."

"And the constellations," Sylvia added because she liked long words. "Especially Leo-the-Lion."

"Wonderful!" Miss Marks said. "Maybe you can tell the class."

So they did. By the time they had finished, Sylvia had forgotten all about being scared of the new school.

Springs and Oceans

O ye Waters that be above the firmament, bless ye the Lord: praise him, and magnify him for ever.

After school Mrs. Kent had snacks ready. While they ate, Jock chattered about all the things he wanted to do. "Let's explore the woods," he said. "Or go climb trees. No, let's find where the brook begins and sail paper boats."

Sylvia made her cookies and milk last as

long as possible. It was warm and cozy in the kitchen. Outdoors it was cold and blowy and there was mud everywhere. "I think I'd rather play with Rosie," she said.

"O.K." Jock hurried toward the door.

"I'll go with you," Seth said and picked up some old newspapers for the boats. "I'll have time before starting my homework."

Suddenly, Sylvia wanted to go along. Seth knew so much. Maybe he'd tell her more about Australia, where Mummy and Daddy were.

"Wait for me. I'll go too." Sylvia ran upstairs for Rosie. When she came down she and Seth followed Jock toward the brook. Jock was way ahead of them, running and jumping over mud puddles.

"How did you like school?" Seth asked.

"Fine. Miss Marks is nice," Sylvia said.

"Hey, that's good," Seth answered.

Soon they reached the brook.

Sylvia had just found a safe place to leave
Rosie when Jock called. "Seth. Syl. Look! I've
found it! The spring that's the beginning of
the brook."

Seth and Sylvia followed Jock up a short
hill. Sylvia saw a trickle of water about the size
of a man's thumb gushing up out of the earth.

"Here's another!" Sylvia said and pointed
to another little spring. "The water keeps on

45

bubbling up like the drinking fountain at school."

Seth called out. "Come look at this. Another spring!"

Jock and Sylvia hurried toward him. They saw that all three springs were close together. The water that gushed out of them joined to make the little brook.

"Just where does all this water come from?" Jock asked as he leaned over to take a closer look.

"From inside the earth. See?" With a stick Seth poked the leaves and stones away from his spring. The water ran out faster than ever. "The water collects underground in little channels until there is so much water it overflows into springs like these."

"Sure, I know that," Jock said, "but what I want to know is where does it come from to get in the earth, and then overflow, and then make a brook? Is it rain?"

"That's right." Seth folded a piece of newspaper into a boat. "The rain runs into the earth and collects in the underground channels."

"But where does the rain come from?" Sylvia wanted to know. "I know it falls from the sky, but how does it get in the sky?"

"You could say the rain starts in brooks," Seth said. "And it starts in rivers and ponds and oceans and every kind of water you can think of. When it's hot and sunny, water is drawn up into the clouds. That's called evaporation."

"E-vap-or-a-tion," Sylvia repeated slowly.
"I like that word."

"Then what happens?" Jock asked.

"When the water cools up there it falls in

raindrops," Seth answered. "And the rain runs into the earth and makes those little underground channels I told you about. It's sort of a circle that goes on and on and on."

Jock and Sylvia were quiet for a moment.

"It's another one of God's great wonders, I guess, isn't it?" Jock said.

"Yes, it is," Seth answered.

"Let's go now," Jock said. "Let's sail our boats."

Sylvia took the boat Seth had made for her and put it into the brook where the water was clearest. The brook ran so fast that in no time at all her boat was out of sight.

"Where will it go?" she asked Seth. "All the way to a river?"

"Your paper boat will sink before it gets to the river," Jock said.

Sylvia didn't listen to him. "Where does the brook go?" she asked Seth. "This brook."

"It runs into the river about three miles from here," Seth said. "And the river runs into the ocean."

Sylvia didn't say a word. She stood looking down at the water flowing along so steadily. As she watched the brook she felt she was part of it and moving with it, on and on and on to the river, then on and on and on to the ocean.

Seth and Jock moved to a place where the brook was deeper, but Sylvia didn't move.

She stood watching the water. Brooks ran into rivers, rivers ran into oceans, and oceans ran together, round and round the earth. Maybe the water in this very brook would go all the way to Australia.

A smile started way down deep inside of

Sylvia. The smile bubbled up and up until it broke out into the happiest kind of laugh. She turned and ran back for Rosie. Sylvia held the Teddy bear over the brook.

"Look, Rosie! Take a good look at the brook."

What a Wonderful World!

O ye Seas and Floods, bless ye the Lord:
praise him, and magnify him for ever.

While Sylvia showed the brook to Rosie, Jock looked for the place where the water ran fastest. He found a very good place. The shallow water rushed by so fast it sang in his ears.

"Here goes!" he called out. "Watch my super-duper jet speed boat."

He pushed his paper boat too hard. The bow dipped and filled with water. The newspaper began to unfold.

"It came apart!" Jock called to Seth as he stared at his sinking boat. "Guess it wasn't any good."

"Make another one," Seth suggested. "Fold the paper tighter and start it off slowly."

Jock leaned over and plunged his arm into the brook. The water was stinging cold. He caught his breath as he pulled the soggy paper toward him. "Boy! That brook's cold. And does it ever run fast!"

"Sure," Seth said. "That's why you have to start a paper boat off slowly and carefully."

Jock hardly heard him. The cold tingling feel of the water on his arm was exciting. It was as exciting as the rushing sound in his ears. "I'm going on down the brook," he said and jumped to his feet.

He hurried along until he came to a small pool. The pool wasn't much bigger than a bath tub. The water was very clear. Jock saw a big shiny rock on the bottom.

"Boy, would I like that for my collection," he said. "Hey, Seth! Syl! Look what I've found."

He reached down with one hand. His sleeve hit the water. As he tried to push it up he lost his balance and started sliding head first toward the water. "Help! Help!" he shouted. Jock's face was nearing the icy water. His hand was numb but he pushed it down toward the shiny rock. He blubbered and snorted as his nose touched the water.

"Help! Seth! Save me!" he called.

Seth ran up and pulled Jock back to the bank. He stood the shivering boy on his feet. "What's the matter with you?" Seth asked. "You're soaked through."

"I—I star—started to f-f-fall." Jock's teeth chattered and he felt very foolish. But he wasn't soaked through as Seth had said. Only half through. One of his legs was wet to the knee and his sleeve was wet and his face was wet. His collar tickled in a clammy way. Jock looked down at his muddy clothes and muddier feet.

"I thought you learned about gravity yesterday," Seth said. "You talked about it enough."

Jock nodded. He felt worse than ever. "There's a rock down there I need for my collection," he explained.

"It will still be there this summer," Seth said. "Now hurry home. Beat it!"

Sylvia heard the shouting and came running up to the boys. She looked at Jock and tried hard not to laugh.

Jock turned for home. It was funny he'd forgotten about gravity. Still, it had worked just the same.

"Hmmm. God's laws are sure terrific!" he said. "I'm glad that gravity always works or else the water in the brook would go all over the place. It'd go over us and over the house and everything! And fall right off the earth. Swish!" Jock laughed.

"You run!" Seth ordered. "Or you'll catch cold and Mum will blame me."

Jock turned and ran. He jumped and bounced as he went. He pretended there wasn't any gravity. Then the brook would come right up and go *splash* down over him! Jock snorted and sniffed and threw up his head. He pretended he was swimming through great enormous splashes of water that went every which way.

When Jock reached the house, he slowed down. He even remembered to take off his muddy boots outside. Indoors the house seemed warm and friendly. Jock scampered upstairs in his socks. Nothing falls off the earth. Nothing! Gravity keeps everything where it belongs— people, brooks, rivers, oceans.

Wow! What a wonderful world!

Lost in the Woods

O all ye Beasts and Cattle, bless ye the Lord:
praise him, and magnify him for ever.

The next few days it rained. Jock and Sylvia could not play out of doors after school. On Friday the rain stopped and the sun came out. Sylvia skipped up the path from the school bus ahead of Jock. Scoop was lying on the big stone door step taking a sun bath. She stooped down to pat him. Scoop's tail pounded up and down. He rolled onto his back, wiggling all over.

Jock scratched the dog's ears. "Scoop's glad to be outside," he said. "He hates rainy days."

"Me too!" Sylvia said. She turned toward the sun with her eyes closed so she could feel the warmth on her face. "Let's go hunt for pussy willows."

"All right," Jock said. "We'll go look in the woods. Scoop can go along. He loves hunting and exploring."

So they started off, with Scoop trotting beside them. Jock wanted to stop and climb trees.

Sylvia shook her head. "I want to find pussy willows. Besides I'm getting cold."

The sun had gone behind a cloud and the air was colder. Jock did some hop-skip-run steps to keep warm. Scoop chased around and then came back.

"Scoop doesn't feel cold," Jock said. "Not ever."

"I do," Sylvia said. "I wish summer would come right away."

"It can't," Jock said and took an extra big jump step. "Don't you remember what Seth said about the North Pole tipping toward the sun? Until that happens, it can't be summer."

Scoop chased after a crow. The crow flew off cawing noisily. Scoop's ears flapped foolishly as he came back to the children. Sylvia laughed at his surprised look. "Dogs can't fly, Scoopie," she said and patted his neck. "They can do lots of things but they can't fly."

Jock ran down the hill toward the woods and Sylvia and Scoop chased after him. The

sun stayed behind the clouds. Inside the woods
it was colder than ever. Sylvia shivered, but
when she saw some pussy willows ahead of her
she forgot about being cold. "These are beautiful big ones!" she said. "Soft as kitten's fur."
She picked a few.

Jock called to her from deeper in the woods.
"Come on over here, Sylvia. I've found some
that are better."

Jock was out of sight and there was no path.
Sylvia hurried toward the sound of his voice,
trying to keep away from the prickly briars.

She wished Jock wouldn't go so deep into the woods and so far away from the path.

"Where are you?" she called.

"Right here," he answered. It sounded far away.

Sylvia ran toward his voice. She was scared and cold. "Are you waiting for me, Jock?" she called.

"Sure I am," he answered. Now his voice was closer.

"Am I glad to find you," Sylvia said when she saw him. "Let's go home. I have enough pussy willows."

"Sure. Sure. Right away," Jock said, but he didn't take a step. When Sylvia turned to look at him he looked away.

"Which way do we go?" she asked. "I'm lost."

"I'm not!" Jock spoke in a loud voice. "At least not really. If it was night I could find the North Star and then I would know which way to go."

"But it isn't night!" Sylvia said. "And I'm cold."

Sylvia and Jock looked around, trying to remember how they had come. They couldn't see the sun, and the big dark tree trunks all looked alike. There seemed to be sticky, pricking briars everywhere. Sylvia gasped with fright when she heard a rustling sound in the underbrush beyond them. She ran to Jock.

"I—I'm sure there aren't any bears in these woods," Jock said and swallowed hard. "B-but I wish the stars would come out so I could find the way home."

"I'm scared," Sylvia whispered.

The rustling noise grew louder and closer.
Sylvia shivered and her teeth rattled. Jock's
face turned white. The noise came nearer and
nearer. Sylvia shut her eyes.

Jock shouted: "It's Scoop! Good old Scoop looking for us."

Sylvia put her arms around Scoop and hid her face in his neck. His soft fur was warm and comforting. Sylvia knew now how they would get home. "Go home, Scoop!" she said. "GO HOME."

"Go home, Scoop," Jock repeated in a shaky voice.

Scoop looked at them, then turned and trotted through the woods. Sylvia and Jock ran after him as fast as they could. Sylvia didn't mind the briars any more. She didn't even notice the pussy willows they passed. Between the trees they saw the field. Jock and Sylvia knew where they were, but they kept on running after Scoop.

"We weren't really lost," Jock said breathlessly when they reached the house. "Because if Scoop hadn't come we could have waited for the stars. God's compass would have showed us the way."

Sylvia patted Scoop. Yes, she thought, and God who made the stars made kind, smart dogs like Scoop, too.

Sylvia Makes a Present

O ye Stars of heaven, bless ye the Lord: praise him,
and magnify him for ever.

One Saturday morning Sylvia helped her aunt
make cookies. "Could I send some to Mummy
and Daddy for Easter, Aunt Matty?" she
asked.

"There isn't time to send them by boat,"

her aunt told her. "And it would cost too much to send them by air. Perhaps you can make something else for them—something light. We could send it off by air mail this afternoon."

Sylvia decided to make a card. She found her paints and began a picture of an Easter lily. It didn't start out very well, but she kept at it.

Jock dashed into the kitchen.

"Where's my baseball bat?" he shouted and joggled Sylvia's arm so she ruined the picture.

"Look!" she said. "Just look what you've done!"

"I'm sorry." Jock stopped short. "Honest, Syl. Can't you make another?"

Sylvia struggled not to cry. "It wasn't any good anyway," she said finally. "I can't paint pictures."

She told Jock about wanting to make something for her mother and father in Australia.

"How about a picture of the Big Dipper and the North Star and Leo?" he suggested. "With all kinds of colors."

Sylvia shook her head. She felt worse than ever. Her paintings never turned out right. She could print well and trace and do neat cutting out, but her painting was always messy.

Jock spouted ideas. Sylvia didn't think any of them were any good until he said: "Why don't you trace a star map out of Seth's star book? After you've traced it onto good paper you can make holes for the stars so the light will shine through. And print in the names."

"I'll trace it onto yellow paper and make green letters," Sylvia said. She went upstairs to find tracing paper and crayons. By the time she came back to the kitchen Jock was gone.

She was sure he had forgotten her, but a moment later he came in carrying a paper chart. His father was with him and Jock was telling him about the Easter card.

"This chart will help you," Jock told Sylvia. "Dr. Gordon lent it to us. Boy, do I wish we owned one."

"Dr. Gordon has invited all of you to look at the stars from his back porch tonight," Mr. Kent said.

"Oh, swell!" Jock said. "He'll tell us lots more about this chart, too. Look, Sylvia, if you turn it you can see how the sky will look any night of the year. Let's turn it to Easter night. You can trace that for your mother and father. Show her, Dad."

"You mean the stars keep changing?" Sylvia asked. "They'll be different on Easter?"

"Yes, Sylvia," Mr. Kent said and set the chart for Easter at eight o'clock in the evening.

Sylvia started tracing. After a little while she looked up. "There are too many stars," she said. "I won't have any room to print the names in green."

"Oh, just put in the best ones," Jock said. "The Big Dipper and the North Star."

"And Leo-the-Lion," Sylvia said. "My favorite."

"Put in Jupiter too!" Jock said. "Because that's a planet, and so is Earth. Boy, Jupiter is bright some nights. And it isn't even a real star, is it, Daddy?"

"No, it's a planet," Mr. Kent said.

"And do the planets travel fast!" Jock began tearing around the kitchen table with his arms outstretched. "I'm the earth traveling around the sun. What's my speed, Dad?"

"Eighteen and a half miles a second," his father said.

"Whew! Here I go," Jock said as he raced around the table.

Sylvia didn't look at him. "Why is the earth called a planet, Uncle John?" she asked.

"The word planet means 'wanderer.' People long ago thought the planets wandered around the sky. They didn't wander really. Each planet follows its own regular path around the sun."

"Like me!" Jock continued to run around the table. "I like to wander. Fast!"

Sylvia was sure Jock would joggle her tracing and ruin it. Luckily Uncle John stopped

him. "You better wander outside where there's more room," he said. "I'll go with you so Sylvia can finish her map in peace."

Jock decided to make an Easter surprise himself. He raced back to the house and borrowed Seth's compass for making circles. He put the star book, crayons, and a big piece of white paper on the kitchen table near Sylvia.

"What are you going to make?" Sylvia asked.

"I'm going to make Mum and Daddy a chart showing Earth and some other planets. I'm even going to put in how far each planet is away from the sun," Jock told her.

First Jock made a big round sun in the middle of the paper. He colored it yellow. Then, working out from the sun he drew in Mercury,

Venus, Earth, Mars, Jupiter, and Saturn. He colored each one. Opening the star book he copied down each planet's distance from the sun. They were so far away it made Jock feel dizzy just to think about it.

Jock showed Sylvia what he had made. "It's pretty, but your letters wobble."

"Mum and Dad will like it," he said as he drew rings around Saturn and put in the earth's moon.

Jock stood off to admire his work. "I know what I'll do," he said. "Under it I'm going to print:

"THE SUN'S FAMILY—HAPPY EASTER"

On Easter Day

O ye Children of Men, bless ye the Lord: praise
him, and magnify him for ever.

During Holy Week everybody in the Kent
household was especially busy. They went to
church all through the week. Then there were

many things to do at home, too, to get ready for Easter.

On Monday Mr. Kent brought home a big mysterious box. It was an Easter present from all the grownups in the parish for Dr. Gordon. By Maundy Thursday Jock was sure he couldn't wait another day to find out what was in the box. Still, it was a secret surprise, and Daddy couldn't tell.

Easter morning was warm and sunny. The Kent family went to church at nine o'clock. When they arrived there was Oliver, Jock's biggest brother, dressed in his sailor's uniform.

"I have a twenty-four hour pass," Oliver said. "I knew you would be coming to church so I came right here."

Mrs. Kent gave him a big hug. "What a wonderful surprise!" she said and turned to

Sylvia. "We like surprises don't we, Sylvia?"

Jock looked at Sylvia and grinned. Yesterday Mum had read a letter from Syl's family. The letter said they had found a house and Sylvia could fly to Australia when school was out. Jock also knew a package had come from Australia. Mum was going to hide it for Sylvia to find in the Easter hunt.

Right now Sylvia and Jock hurried to put on their choir robes. They were in the junior choir.

When it came to the sermon it seemed as though Dr. Gordon was talking just to the Kents, although he was looking at everyone.

"I note," he said "that Easter is beginning to be like Christmas with many gifts passing back and forth."

Jock looked down from the choir and caught

his father looking at him. Did Dr. Gordon
know about the gift he was getting?

"And this is right," went on Dr. Gordon,

"for we have reason today to be thankful. The same God who made the stars and the planets died for us and conquered death."

Jock was not sure he understood what Dr. Gordon was saying. He did know about the Cross and the empty Easter tomb, but he wondered just how God did it. Well, anyway, now he saw something about Easter that he had not seen before. God was sure powerful to make the heavens and also conquer death.

By the time Jock began listening again, Dr. Gordon was talking very slowly and sort of very seriously so Jock knew the sermon was just about over.

"My Gift to you today," said Dr. Gordon, "is a Gift I did not buy, but one that was given to me and that we can give to each other. I give you Jesus Christ who rose from the dead and is your King in glory."

Then Dr. Gordon turned and everybody stood. Jock was still thinking. He could not remember ever having thought about a sermon before. In fact, he usually wasn't listening, but this one was different.

Was Jesus Christ up in the sky? What was "glory"? Well, anyway, He was a king, and Jock felt the same way about Him that he did about the God who made the stars.

That afternoon Sylvia was still acting as though she were in the choir as they waited for the Easter hunt to begin.

"Come, ye faithful, raise the strain of triumphant gladness," Sylvia sang. She started on the second verse:

" 'Tis the spring of souls today;
    Christ hath burst his prison,
  And from three days' sleep in death
    As a sun hath risen.' "

"So you know all the words!" Oliver smiled at Sylvia. "That's more than I did when I was in junior choir. Mum wrote me that you've learned a lot of star names too."

"So have I!" Jock began. Just then Mum
called to them from the lawn that the Easter
hunt was ready.

Jock found dyed eggs and jelly beans and

cookies. Sylvia found the same things and the package from Australia. It was a toy koala bear that looked like a live one. For a minute Jock wished someone had sent him a koala bear. Then he remembered he hadn't hidden his planet present for Mum and Dad.

"Shut your eyes!" he said and dashed around the lawn to find a good place to hide it. He finally decided on the biggest lilac bush. It turned out to be a good place. Jock had to give Mum and Dad hints about being hot and cold before Mum finally found it.

"Why it's beautiful, Jock." Mum looked pleased. "You must have worked awfully hard over it."

Dad looked at it over Mum's shoulder. "All of us are star minded," he said, "but I think we will be more so with the present the parish gave Dr. Gordon."

"What is it?" Jock's curiosity fizzled up inside of him. "You promised you would tell us on Easter."

"It's a telescope!" Dad said. "A 150-power telescope. That means if you look at Leo-the-Lion or any other stars through it, they will seem 150 times nearer to you."

"But Dad, do you think Dr. Gordon will like his present?"

"Why not?" said Dad.

"I don't know," Jock said. "He said something this morning about giving us a king."

"You are right, Jock," Dad said. "Our gift doesn't compare with his, but I think he will like it."

"Of course," said Mum. "With this telescope
he can look at what the King has made."

Oliver walked over to Jock. "I've hidden

something for you," he said. "It's something I
think you'll like. I'll give you a hint. It's about
things that are high and it's hidden high."

Jock looked up until his neck ached. Finally he saw something in the crotch of the apple tree. He ran toward it, Sylvia and Scoop following him.

"I'm taller!" Sylvia said. "Maybe I can reach it."

"I can climb!" Jock said. A moment later he stood on the ground holding a star-finder chart. It was just like the one he had borrowed from Dr. Gordon.

"Is it mine for keeps?" Jock asked. Oliver nodded, and Jock felt shivery with excitement. He would use the star finder tonight. Then when they visited Dr. Gordon he could see the stars that were on it through a real telescope!

"You bet it's yours," Oliver said. "I sent away to the Planetarium for it. From what Mum wrote it seems to me you might be an astronomer."

Jock couldn't say a word. He turned the chart slowly. The little stars moved from east to west the way they really seemed to do at night. As he watched he smiled to himself. The stars and the planets were different.

So were people when you came to think of it. Sylvia liked to set the table and pick pussy willows. He liked to run around and climb trees and stuff.

Jock felt happy with a special Easter happiness. He knew now, so that he felt it right up from his toes, that this earth was God's. Even though everybody was different there was a place for him and for everyone.

He couldn't stand still. He gave Mum the star finder to hold while he tried to do cartwheels across the lawn. Upside or downside, God's world was wonderful.

Selected Verses

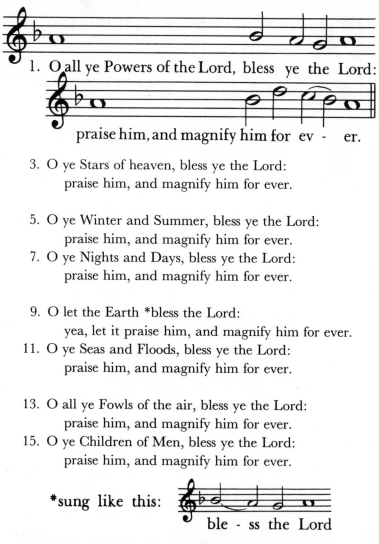

1. O all ye Powers of the Lord, bless ye the Lord:
   praise him, and magnify him for ev - er.

3. O ye Stars of heaven, bless ye the Lord:
   praise him, and magnify him for ever.

5. O ye Winter and Summer, bless ye the Lord:
   praise him, and magnify him for ever.
7. O ye Nights and Days, bless ye the Lord:
   praise him, and magnify him for ever.

9. O let the Earth *bless the Lord:
   yea, let it praise him, and magnify him for ever.
11. O ye Seas and Floods, bless ye the Lord:
   praise him, and magnify him for ever.

13. O all ye Fowls of the air, bless ye the Lord:
   praise him, and magnify him for ever.
15. O ye Children of Men, bless ye the Lord:
   praise him, and magnify him for ever.

*sung like this:

ble - ss the Lord

The music used here is adapted from chant 629, The Hymnal 1940.

from the Benedicite

T. T. Noble

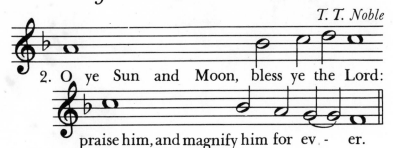

2. O ye Sun and Moon, bless ye the Lord:
praise him, and magnify him for ev - er.

4. O ye Showers and Dew, bless ye the Lord:
   praise him, and magnify him for ever.

6. O ye Ice and Snow, bless ye the Lord:
   praise him, and magnify him for ever.

8. O ye Light and Darkness, bless ye the Lord:
   praise him, and magnify him for ever.

10. O ye Mountains and Hills, bless ye the Lord:
    praise him, and magnify him for ever.

12. O ye Whales, and all that move in the waters, bless ye the Lord:
    praise him, and magnify him for ever.

14. O all ye Beasts and Cattle, bless ye the Lord:
    praise him, and magnify him for ever.

16. Let us bless the Father, and the Son, and the *Holy Ghost:
    praise him, and magnify him for ever.

*sung like this: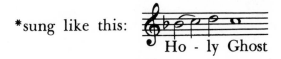

The complete canticle will be found on page 11 of the Book of Common Prayer.

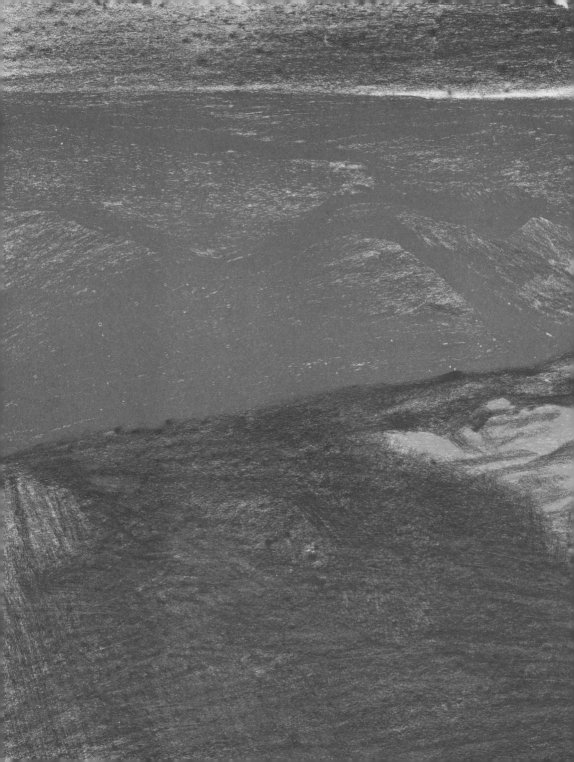